Scott & Emmy
Fullerton

THIS BOOK BELONGS TO:

WHO IS A VERY SPECIAL PERSON TO:

www.mascotbooks.com

DON'T SAY GATOR

©2023 Douglas Killingtree. All Rights Reserved. No part of this publication may be reproduced, stored in a retrieval system or transmitted in any form by any means electronic, mechanical, or photocopying, recording or otherwise without the permission of the author.

For more information, please contact
Mascot Kids, an imprint of Amplify Publishing Group:
620 Herndon Parkway #220
Herndon, VA 20170
info@mascotbooks.com

Library of Congress Control Number: 2023901489
CPSIA Code: PRKF0223A
ISBN-13: 978-1-63755-663-4

Printed in China

DON'T SAY GATOR

written & illustrated by douglas killingtree

scan the QR to watch the video & sing along!

DONTSAYGATOR.COM

music by corinne sharlet
animated by jeremey morales vii

For you.

You're great.

I've never really been the sort
to cause a lot of trouble.

I do my homework and play nice
inside my rainbow bubble!

But sometimes simply being you is too much for some people,

and 'cause they don't like THEMSELVES, they make being you ILLEGAL!

Well, guess what?

I'm ME!

Exactly who I'm SUPPOSED to be!

And I see people everyday expressing LOVE in their own way, who aren't afraid to stand and saaay . . .

I'm GAAAAAA

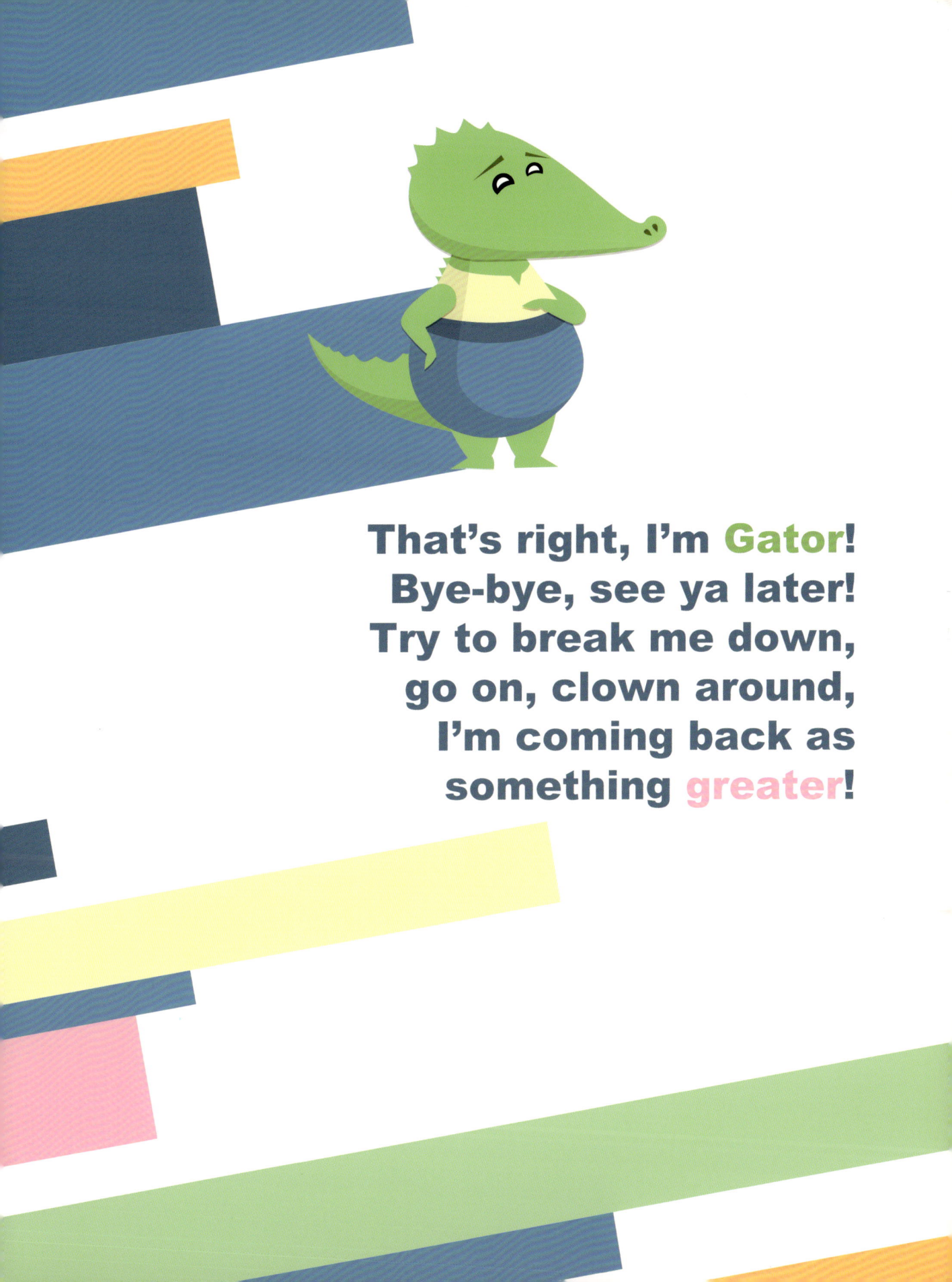

That's right, I'm Gator!
Bye-bye, see ya later!
Try to break me down,
go on, clown around,
I'm coming back as
something greater!

If you don't like the way I am, bye-bye see ya later!
I won't suffer no haters!

I've always known who I was from the moment that I **hatched**. And that the person who I am never really matched

the person everybody else expected me to be.

Well guess what? Who cares? I make no apologies!

"But why can't you,"
they ask and ask,
"just be a crocodile?"

I hoped
and wished
to change who I was
for a while.

But have you ever
really tried,
being something
that you're not?
Good luck! Nice try!
It really takes a lot!

I get it, I guess . . .
You want things to stay the same,

but then you lost me
when you said I can't speak my name . . .

Alright then,
two can play that game!

I'm Gator, I'm Gator!
Bye-bye, see ya later!
You'll never break me,
never make me
into someone straighter.

It's taken me so many years
to finally understand
I will not, cannot change,
no matter the demand.

So if you say I cannot speak
this word I know I am,
what choice have I but to disobey
and shuffle off this sham?

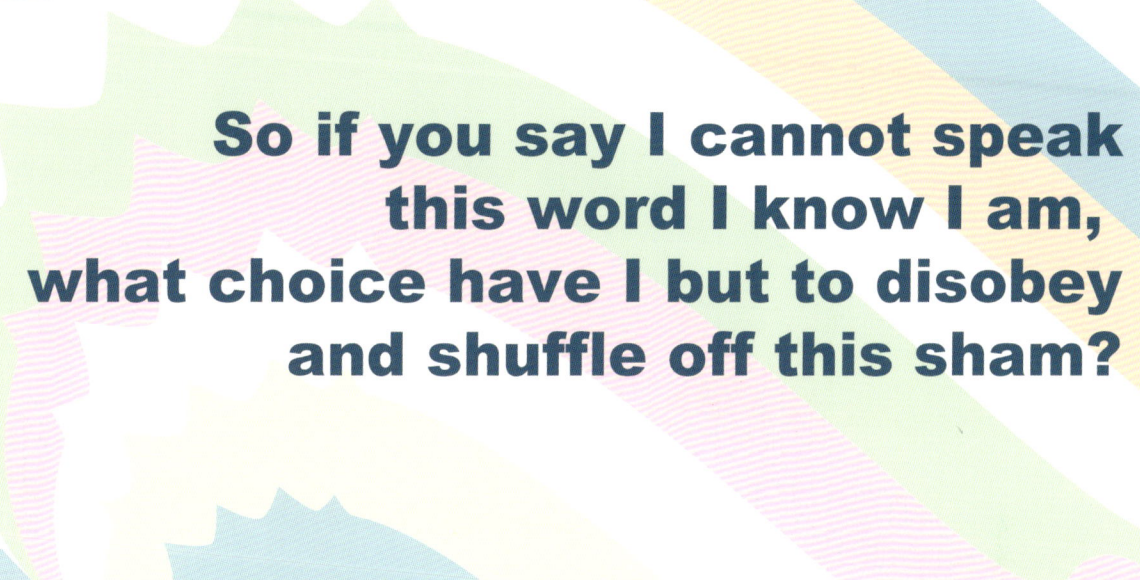

**Remember: always be yourself,
and someday you will see,
the people who matter most
love you
unconditionally!**

fabulous

**And they'll be proud!
I'm so proud!
When you say out loud,
I'll say it loud!**

I'm Gator! (Say Gator!) Bye-bye, see ya later!
I'm getting stronger, laughing longer,
au revoir, my haters!

I'm Gator, I'm Gator!
Bye-bye, see ya later!
I'm getting stronger (getting stronger),
laughing longer (laughing longer),
auf Wiedersehen, mein Haters!

So to all the other gators
out in the Everglades,
know there's someone just like you
who sings this serenade...

I'm Gator, I'm Gator!
I hope to see you later!
You're not alone
   or on your own,
      your love just makes you greater.

To the Queer Kids of Florida & Beyond . . .

A whole bunch of people from all over the United States helped make this book FOR YOU. Together they raised $10,000 so that YOU could have this book. So that you would know that they love you ***just as you are.***

You've been on Earth your whole life, and in that time it must seem like things have only gotten worse. But I promise you **things will get better**. Those same people who helped make this book for you are working with a whole bunch of other people to create a world where everyone can just be who they are, no more having to hide or feel alone.

In the meantime, be safe, be kind, do your homework, have fun, and if anyone tries to make you feel bad about who you are . . . *"Bye-bye, see ya later!"*

Resources

THE TREVOR PROJECT | thetrevorproject.org

Our favorite non-profit . . . The Trevor Project is the leading national organization providing crisis intervention and suicide prevention services to LGBTQ+ young people, ages 13-24. They also provide excellent resources and training for parents and educators.

IF YOU NEED HELP URGENTLY, PLEASE CALL THE TREVOR PROJECT LIFELINE AT 1-866-488-7386.

IT GETS BETTER PROJECT | itgetsbetter.org

The It Gets Better Project was created to show young LGBTQ+ people the levels of happiness, potential, and positivity their lives will reach—if they can just get through their teen years. The It Gets Better Project wants to remind teenagers in the LGBTQ+ community that they are not alone—and it WILL get better.

QUEER KIDS' STUFF | queerkidstuff.com

This webseries aims to eliminate stigma by educating future generations through entertaining video content. Creator and host Lindsay and their best stuffed friend, Teddy, explain queer topics through a vlog-style conversation with young viewers focused on love and family. The short videos are a tool for parents, teachers, and LGBTQ+ adults to help them explain these words and ideas to young children in their lives, recommended for ages three and up.

Special Thanks

My dear friends
Scott & Emily,
for their incredible support (and food).

My best friend
Sasha,
with whom I can be completely myself.

My siblings
Jeri, Jessi, and Sam,
for their unconditional love.

My patient, kind, and caring partner
Calvin,
without whom I would be utterly lost.

And of course
Lynette Jett
and all our generous
Kickstarter supporters!

DOUGLAS KILLINGTREE | Author & Illustrator

Born and raised in Chugiak, Alaska, Douglas (nee Reynolds) is a BFA theater arts alum from Southern Oregon University. His previous works include *A Normal Turtle* and *An Actual Family*, with a fourth book, *Every Witch Way*, in pre-production.

He lives in Portland, Oregon, with his partner, Calvin, and their Rhodesia Boxer, Harper.

CORINNE SHARLET | Composer

Corinne Sharlet is a singer-songwriter and psychotherapist based in Portland, Oregon. She has performed both locally and on tour. Her new album, *A Lovely Future*, is out now on corinnesharlet.com

With her own songs being poetic and often emotionally raw, Corinne was the clear choice to bring Lil Gator's anthem to life. She hopes to work on more children's music in the future!

Photo by Courtney Hellen Photography

JEREMY MORALLES VII | Animator

Jeremy is a graphic designer and illustrator who enjoys using design as a storytelling tool. He previoiusly animated the musical version of *A Normal Turtle* for 5th Avenue Theatre. Jeremy is an award-winning artist who has worked with Broadway Across America and the Seattle Children's Hospital.

He lives and works as a freelance artist in Seattle, Washington.

Lil Gator likes to express themself in different ways.

Why not draw on some make-up for them?

What color should their scarf, dress, shoes, hair, and clutch be?

Try adding some jewelry!

With the help of an adult, you can cut out your own Lil Gator!